E.P.L.

D0603248

oval and square

rectangles

rectangle

oval

circles

line

oval

rectangles

rectangle

ovals

rectangle

lines

oval

lines

lines

rectangles

rectangle

lines

circle

oval

circle and oval

lines

Robot Zombie
Franken

For Brenda, Mary Lee, and always, Kent—
superheroes in disguise

Copyright © 2012 by Annette Simon

All rights reserved. No part of this book may be reproduced, transmitted, or stored in an information
retrieval system in any form or by any means, graphic, electronic, or mechanical, including photocopying,
taping, and recording, without prior written permission from the publisher.

First edition 2012

Library of Congress Cataloging-in-Publication Data is available.

Library of Congress Catalog Card Number pending

ISBN 978-0-7636-5124-4

CCP 17 16 15 14 13 12
10 9 8 7 6 5 4 3 2 1

Printed in Shenzhen, Guangdong, China

This book was typeset in Officina Sans.
The illustrations were created digitally in QuarkXPress.

Candlewick Press
99 Dover Street
Somerville, Massachusetts 02144

visit us at www.candlewick.com

stein!

Annette Simon

CANDLEWICK PRESS

Robot.

Robot.

Robot?

Robot ZOMBIE!

Yikes. Robot reboot. . . .

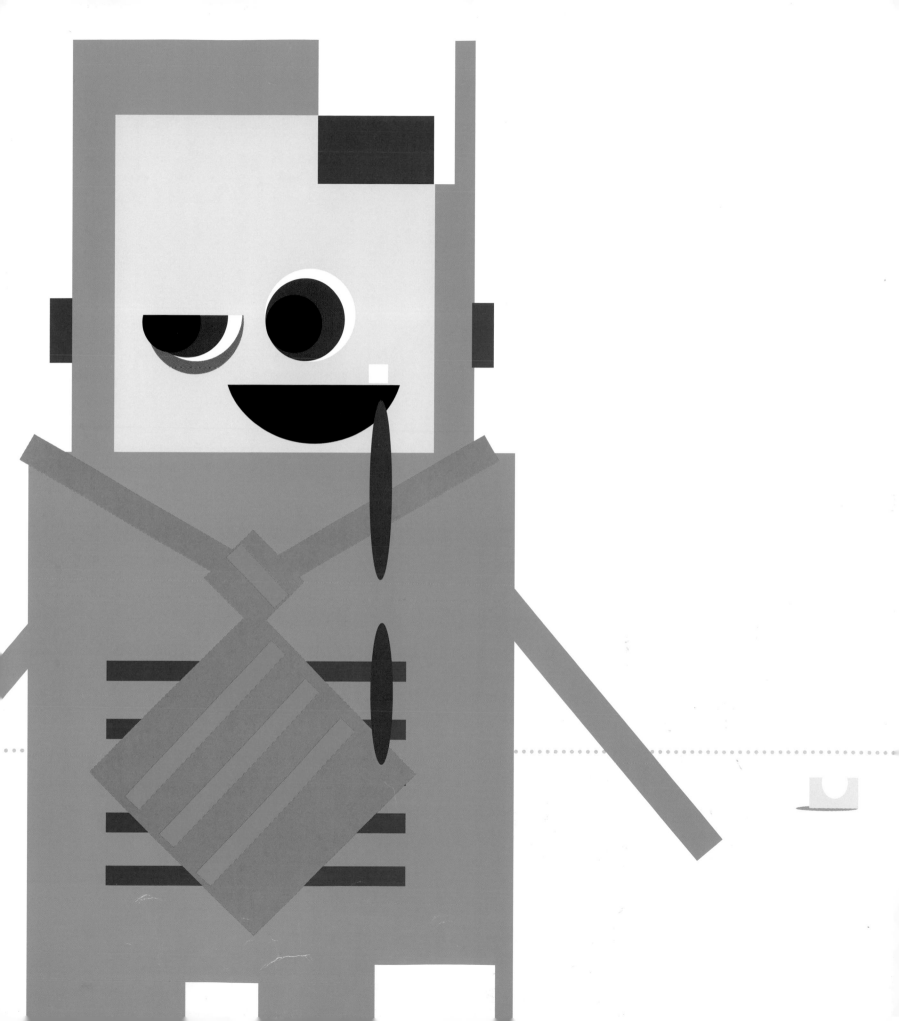

Robot zombie
Frankenst

ein!

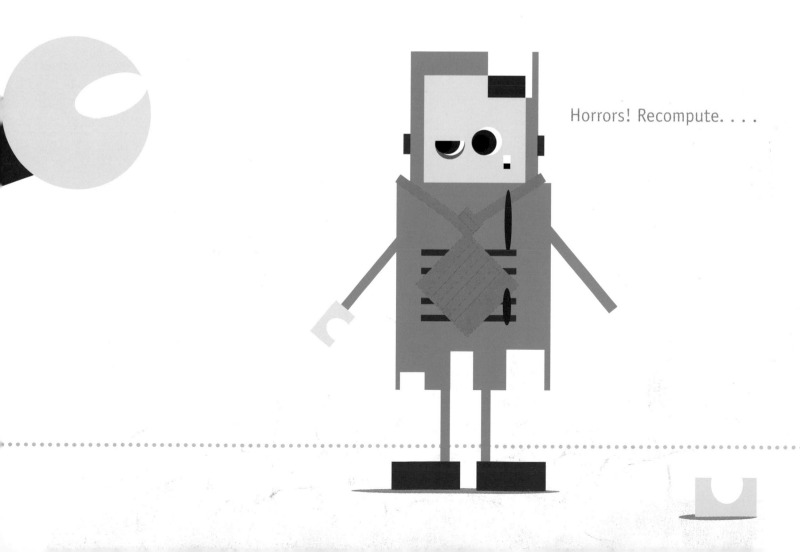

Horrors! Recompute. . . .

Robot zombie
Frankenstein
PIRATE!

Arrr, a scallywag . . .

Robot zombie
Frankenstein
pirate
superhero!

Super TRICKSTER! Hmmm . . .

Robot zombie Frankenstein pirate superhero.

In disguise!

Super trickster-ER!

Robot zombie Frankenstein pirate superhero-in-disguise OUTER SPACE INVADER!

Blasting off in 3 . . . 2 . . . 1 . . .

Robot zombie
Frankenstein pirate supe
outer space
CH

hero-in-disguise
invader

EF!

. . . with pie!

. . . with FORK!

Robot . . .

buddies?

Mmm . . .

affirmative!

striped tie

robot mouth

pirate hook

robot face

robot foot

nose disguise

zombie drool

robot chest panel

eyeball

robot torso

robot knob

robot hand

robot base

zombie eyeball

outer space invader helmet

pirate eye patch

Frankenstein bolt

robot head

robot chest panel